THE TALON & THE BLADE

PRAISE FOR JASMINE SILVERA

"DEATH'S DANCER weaves suspense and romance into a story as smart as it is sensual... Silvera deftly choreographs the action using lush depictions of Prague's storied scenery and deliciously dark humor. A thrilling debut." -Camille Griep, *Letters to Zell, New Charity Blues*

"A spirited, sexy paranormal romance." -Kirkus Reviews (Death's Dancer)

ALSO BY JASMINE SILVERA

Death's Dancer (Grace Bloods #1)

Best Served Cold (Short Story)

Dancer's Flame (Grace Bloods #2)